Published 2002 by Tucker Slingsby Ltd

This US edition produced for Borders Group, Inc.

This Canadian edition produced for Indigo Books & Music Inc.

Devised and produced by Tucker Slingsby Ltd
Roebuck House, 288 Upper Richmond Road West
London SW14 7JG, England

Illustrations by Jan Lewis
Copyright © illustrations and text Tucker Slingsby Ltd 1995, 1998, 1999 and 2002
Copyright © this edition Tucker Slingsby Ltd 2002

ISBN 1-902272-21-8

Manufactured in Singapore by Imago

1 2 3 4 5 6 7 8 9 06 05 04 03 02

Color reproduction by Bright Arts Graphics, Singapore

My Big Book of
Fairy Tales
and Rhymes

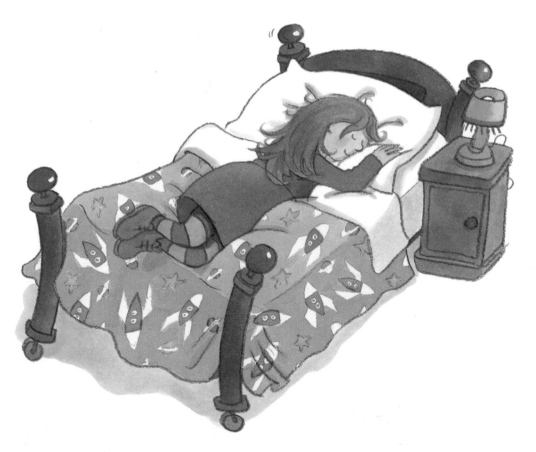

In this book

THIS LITTLE PIG

This little pig

Went to market.

This little pig

stayed
at
home.

This little pig

had roast

beef,

"This little

pig had none.

and this
little pig ...

...Went ee ee eo

all the way home.

This little
mouse appears
13 times in the story of
The Ugly Duckling.
Can you spot him?

The Ugly Duckling

Mother duck sits on her nest,
For her eggs she does her best.

Ducklings hatch, what a lot!
Five are fluffy, one is not.

He is scruffy, big and brown,
Scrawny neck, no yellow down.

Ducklings peck him. "Go away.
We think you're ugly," they all say.

Off he swims to some far lake,
Feeling that his heart will break.

Crying great big tears, he glides
Behind the reeds and sadly hides.

Summer passes, cold winds blow.
Winter comes with ice and snow.

Soon the lake begins to freeze
And our duckling starts to sneeze.

Lonely, cold, with frozen feet,
He grows thin—no food to eat.

Then the warm Spring comes at last.
The sun is hot, the ice melts fast.

Ugly Duckling
looks up to the sky,
Sees three white
swans flying by.

He flaps his wings and, with a cry,
Soon he is flying fast and high.

On the pond the three swans land.
Heads held high, they're very grand.

Ugly Duckling lands close by,
Feeling scared and very shy.

But the swans all say, "Hi!
What a very handsome guy!"

As they swim in his direction,
He looks down at his reflection.

In the water, shining bright,
He sees a swan, all smooth and white.

"I'm no duckling! From now on,
I'm a fine but modest swan."

By the pond, the children call,
"There's a new swan, best of all."

Happy with his new swan friends,
So the duckling's story ends.

A little caterpillar
appears 9 times in the
story of
Little Red Riding Hood.
Can you spot him
creeping along?

Little Red Riding Hood

Dear Little Red Riding Hood
Lived very close to a big, dark wood.

"Will you please,"
her mother said,
"Take this to Granny
who's sick in bed."

With the food, Red Riding Hood
Walked into the big, dark wood.

Soon a huge wolf stopped her walk.
Grinning, he said, "Let's have a talk."

"Where are you going?" the big wolf cried.
"To see my Granny," Little Red replied.

"And Mother said I never should
Speak to strangers in the wood!"

Off raced the wolf—he'd made a plan.
To Granny's house he swiftly ran.

He rushed straight in, with open jaws,
And swallowed Granny without pause.

Then, with Granny's nightcap and gown,
Into the bed he snuggled down.

Soon Red Riding Hood came in.
She stood and stared at Granny's grin.

"What big eyes you have," she said.
"The better to see you!" said Wolf in bed.

"What big ears you have," said she.
"To hear you loud and clear!" said he.

"What big teeth you have," she sighed.
"All the better to eat you with!" he cried.

He gulped her down, then closed his jaw,
Back in bed, began to snore.

In the forest, a woodcutter heard
One faint scream.
Was that a bird?

"Best to see all's well with Gran."
To the cottage
he quickly ran.

When he saw the wolf in bed,
With one blow he killed it dead.

Out popped Granny, Little Red too,
A tiny bit squashed, but good as new!

"Oh dear," said Granny, "What a fuss!
Thanks so much for saving us."

Then the happy, thankful three,
All sat down to cakes and tea.

Lots of little mice appear in this story of **Cinderella**. There are 19 altogether. Can you spot them all?

Cinderella

Cinderella, kind and sweet,
Wore old clothes and had bare feet.

Her *two* stepsisters were ugly and mean.
Her stepmother was a horrid old bean.

They made her work all through the day,
With not much food and, of course, no pay.

Then a footman brought by hand,
Three printed cards, all very grand.

To *the* ball *the* uglies were invited,
They laughed and screamed, so excited!

Came the day, the sisters dressed
In new clothes, their very best.

Cinderella sat alone to cry.
Heard a voice, saw something fly.

It was her fairy godmother, who said,
"You'll go *to* the ball, not stay here in bed!"

She waved her wand, a flash of light,
Cinderella's dress was new and bright.

Cinderella set off in her new frock.
She promised to be back by *twelve o'clock*.

Cinderella, at the ball all night,
Danced with the prince, such delight.

Then the clock struck twelve.
"Oh, no!"
Cried Cinderella,
"Now I must go."

Out she ran and lost one shoe.
In her old clothes home she flew.

Next day, the prince said, "Now, who
Is the girl who wore this shoe?"

Every girl, short, fat, thin, tall,
Tried on the shoe. It was too small.

An ugly sister did just manage,
To push in a *toe*, causing great damage!

When Cinderella tried on the little shoe,
Of course it fit her right and true.

"At last I've found you!" the prince said. He kissed her hand. "Now let us wed."

Cinderella laughed and said, "Yes, please."
She gave his hand a little squeeze.

At the wedding, song and laughter,
And they lived happily ever after.

A little black bird
appears 9 times in the
story of
The Three Little Pigs.
Can you spot him
every time?

The Three Little Pigs

"Oh my dears," said Mother Pig,
"You three pigs have grown quite big."

"Now that you are almost grown,
Build new houses of your own."

"Off you go, but just watch out.
The big, bad wolf roams here about."

The first pig built his house of straw,
With two fine windows and a door.

With some sticks the second pig
Built a house, quite grand and big.

The third pig
worked hard for days,
Using bricks
in clever ways.

He built a house with walls and roof,
Windows, chimney—all wolf-proof!

Then Wolf growled at the house of straw,
"Let me in!" He licked his paw.

"Just go away," the first pig said.
"I'm not scared, I'm safe in bed."

The wolf huffed and puffed and blew
The straw house down. Out Pig flew.

First Pig ran just as fast as he could,
Straight to the little house made of wood.

But soon the wolf knocked and growled,
"Let me in." "No!" two pigs howled.

The wolf huffed and puffed and blew
The stick house down, flat and true.

The two pigs dodged the wolf's great jaws,
Ran to the brick house, locked the doors.

The wolf huffed and puffed and blew
At the brick house, strong and new.

When he had used up all his puff,
He knew the house was just too tough.

Angry, onto the roof he nipped
And down the chimney quickly slipped.

The pigs were ready with a pot,
Full of water, boiling hot.

When the wolf into it slid,
They put on the heavy lid.

Three little pigs danced and said,
"Safe at last, the wolf is dead!"

aye - oh!

And on that farm

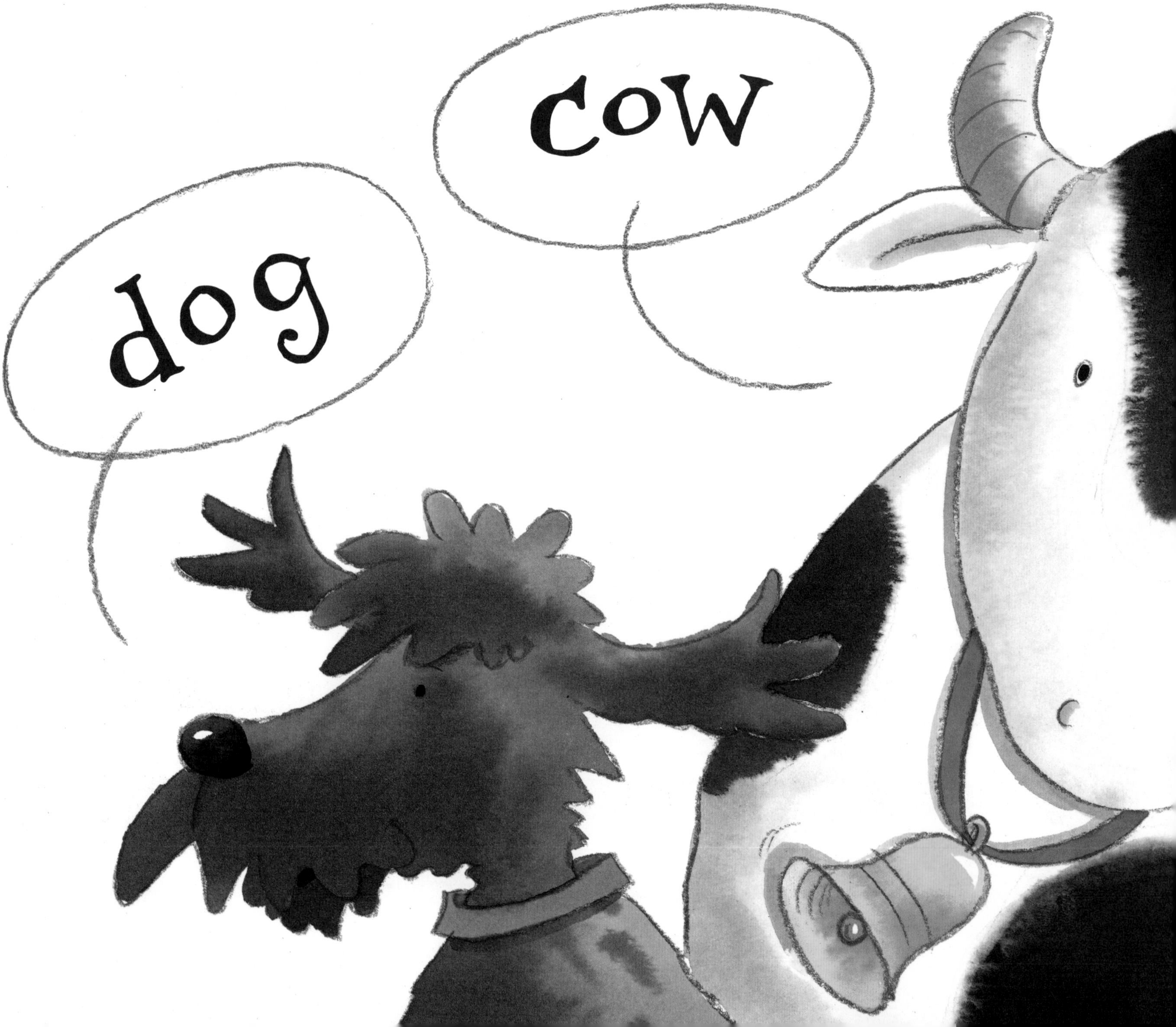

Ee-aye-ee

aye-oh!

and a

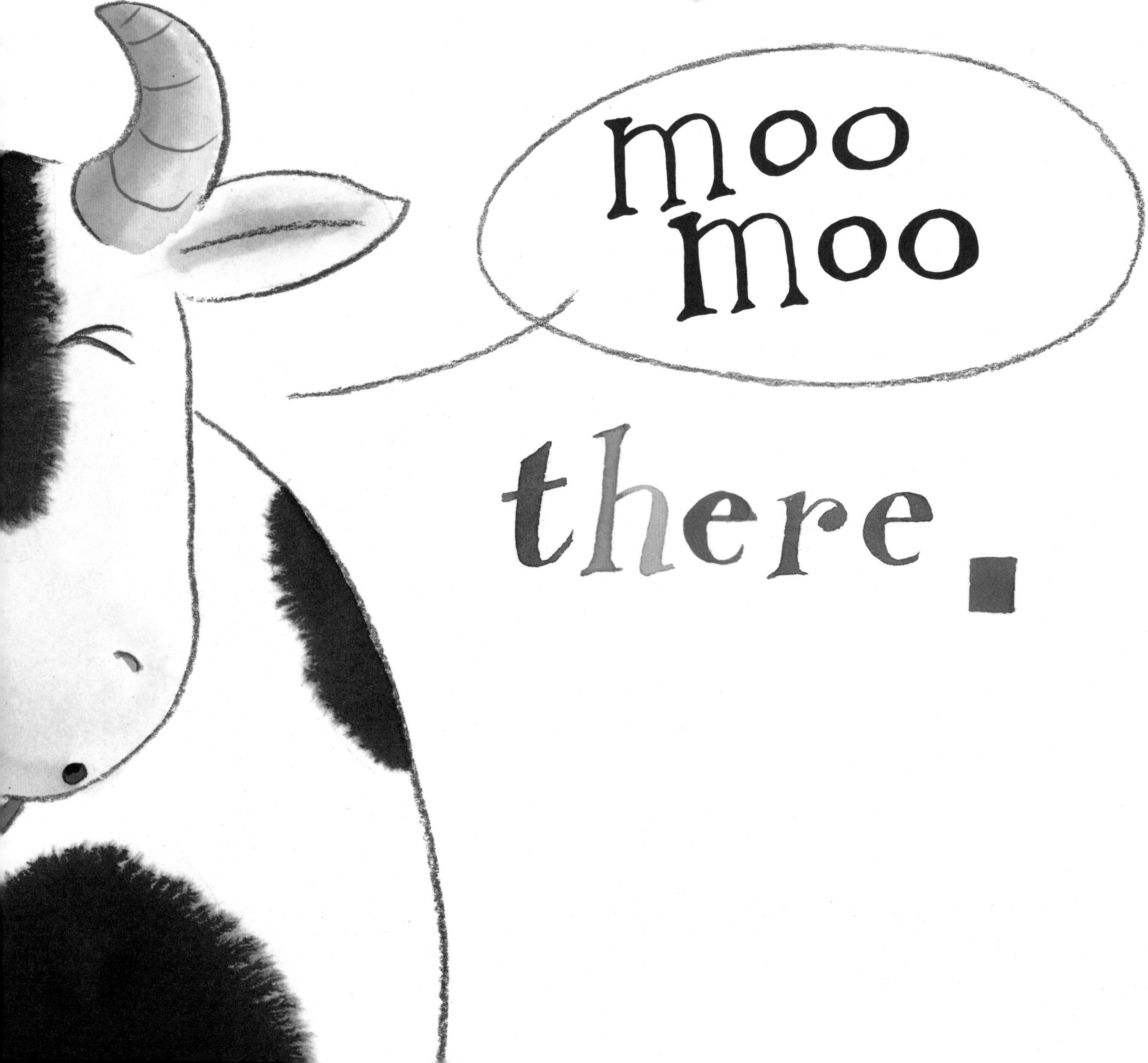

there.

And a

woof woof

here...

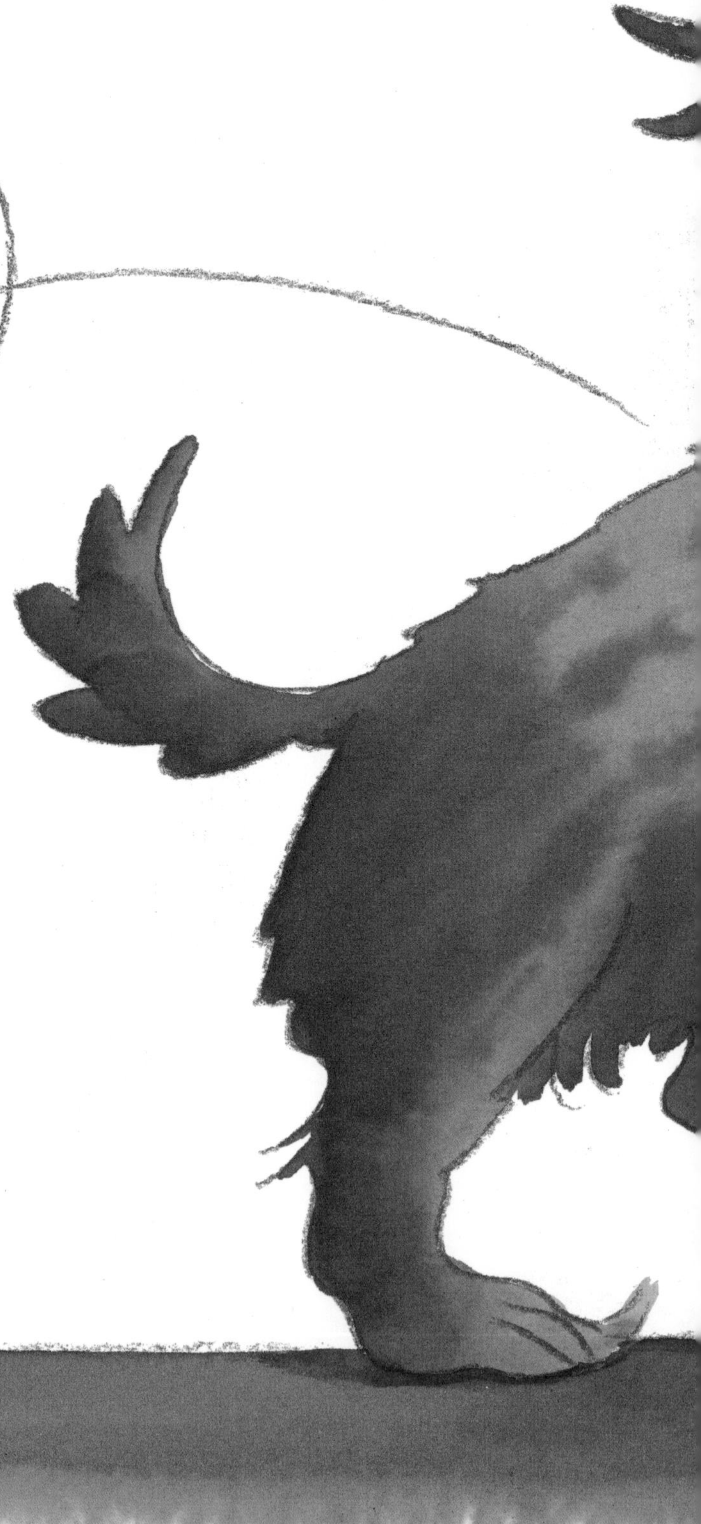

and a

Woof Woof

there.

'Here a

baa

there a

baa

'Here a

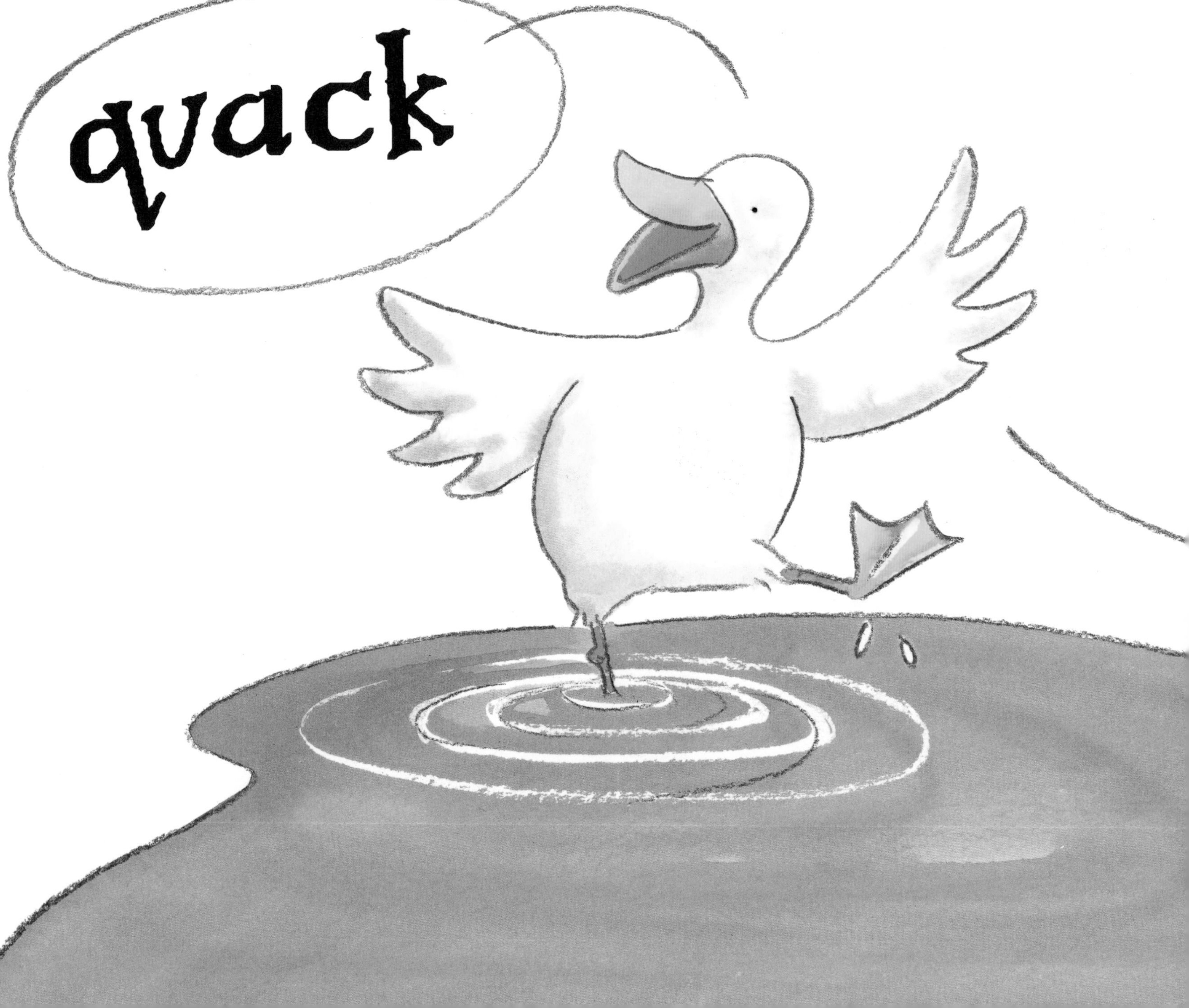

there a

quack

Old Macdonald
Ee-aye-ee -

had a farm,
aye-oh!

Can you
find 11 pictures of
this little blue bird
in the story?

Sleeping Beauty

A new baby for the Queen and King!
They planned a special christening.

Good fairies flew in from all over the place
With magic gifts: wealth, beauty, and grace.

But the wicked fairy brought only tears.
"She'll prick her finger and sleep for years!"

Needles and pins were banned straight away.
Beauty was safe and more lovely each day.

The King sent word: "Come one, come all!
Come to Beauty's seventeenth birthday ball."

The bad fairy hid in the palace tower,
Well disguised by her magic power.

Beauty found her there, busily spinning,
"Try this, my dear," she croaked, grinning.

When Beauty touched the spinning wheel
It pricked her finger and she gave a squeal.

At once Beauty fell fast asleep,
And everyone in the palace started to weep.

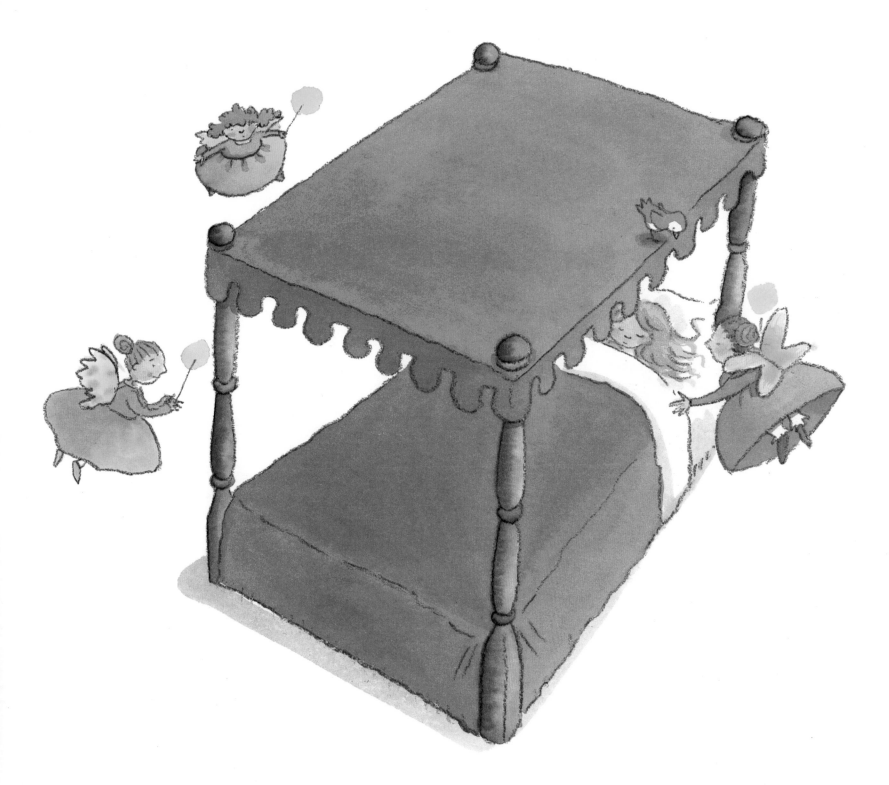

Kind fairies could not undo the spell
So they put everyone else to sleep as well.

Around the palace, the trees grew high.
Nothing stirred until a prince rode by.

He'd heard about the wicked fairy
And decided to visit although it was scary!

Sword in hand, he cut his way through.
It took him hours and he got scratched too!

Inside *the* palace he looked everywhere,
Found Beauty asleep and stopped *to* stare.

"What a lovely girl," he said,
And gently kissed her on the head.

Beauty woke up with a start,
Smiled at the Prince with a happy heart.

The Prince had broken the wicked spell.
Soon everyone else was awake as well.

The Queen invited the Prince to stay,
And what a feast they had that day!

The Prince asked Beauty if they could wed,
She laughed and smiled, "Yes, let's," she said.

Beauty married her handsome prince.
They haven't seen the bad fairy since.

Can you
find 9 pictures of
this pair of mice
in the story?

Goldilocks and the Three Bears

Father, Mother, and Baby—the Three Bears
Sat down to breakfast in their chairs.

"This porridge is too hot to eat,"
Said Father Bear, getting to his feet.

"Let's take a walk while we wait."
So the Three Bears went to the garden gate.

Along comes Goldilocks, who then sees
The little house among the trees.

She knocked on the door. No one within.
The naughty girl just walked right in.

She took a spoon and made a hole
In the porridge in Father's bowl.

"Much *too hot*," she screamed and tried Mother's bowl, "Too cool," she cried.

She tried the smallest bowl, and soon
Ate it all and licked the spoon.

First she sat in the great big chair.
It belonged to Father Bear.

Then she tried the middle chair.
It belonged to Mother Bear.

The smallest chair seemed to be just right.
But it broke and gave her an awful fright.

Full of porridge and wanting to sleep,
Into the bedroom she did creep.

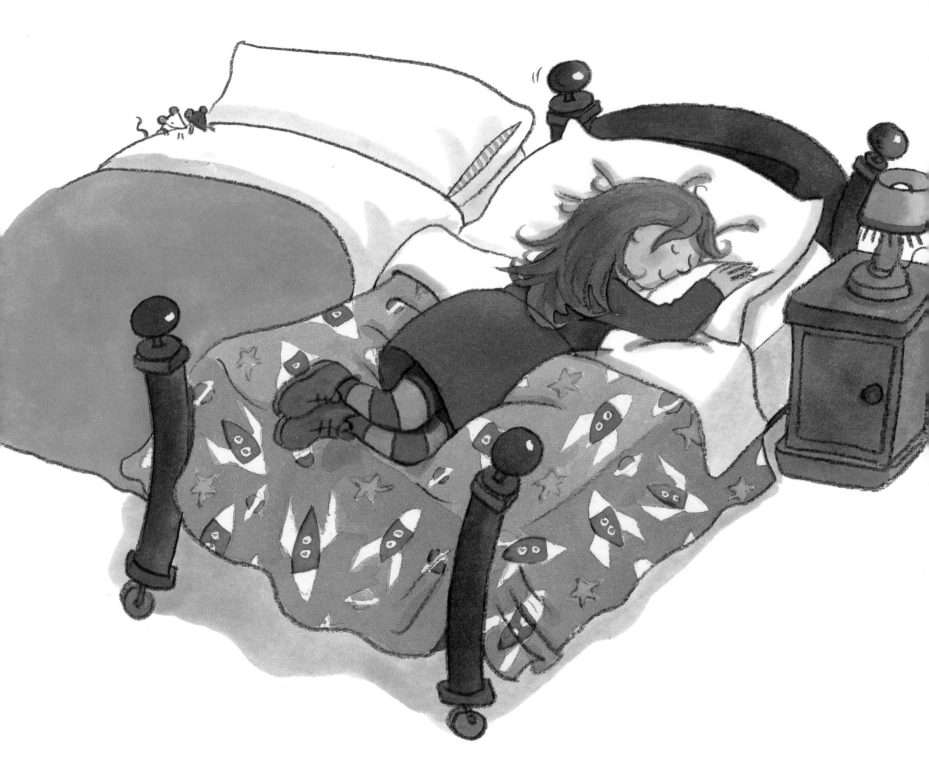

She tried three beds, the smallest was best,
So she snuggled down for a little rest.

Soon the bears came through the door,
Very puzzled at what they saw.

"Someone's been here," Father growled.
"They've eaten my porridge," Baby howled.

"And look at *that*," cried Baby Bear,
"They've broken up my little chair."

Baby Bear trotted off to his bed,
Saw on the pillow a golden head.

"There she is," cried Baby Bear.
"She ate my porridge and broke my chair."

Goldilocks woke up in such a fright.
The angry bears were a scary sight!

She jumped through the window, over the sill,
And for all we know, she's running still.

Can you
find 11 pictures of
Aladdin's cat
in *this* story?

Aladdin and *the* Magic Lamp

Aladdin, a very poor and ragged boy,
Was his mother's pride and joy.

They had little food and no money at all.
Then a long lost uncle came to call!

He took Aladdin out for a walk.
By a dark cave, he stopped to talk.

"Inside *this* cave, there's a lamp on *the* floor. Please fetch it for me—I can't get in the door."

Deep in the cave was treasure galore!
Al found the lamp and made for the door.

"Hand over the lamp, or I'll slit your gizzard."
This was no uncle, but an evil wizard!

Aladdin refused, which made Wizard wild. "I'm locking you in, you horrible child."

"What should I do? How can I leave?"
Al sat, rubbing the lamp with his sleeve.

A genie shot out, saying "Can I help, Master?"
"Take me back home, and fast if not faster!"

With a flash and a bang Aladdin arrived.
His mother was really very surprised!

"Now genie," said Al,
"I'd like some more wishes,
Money, a palace, and food on gold dishes."

Al wanted these riches to help him impress
A charming and very pretty princess.

The princess liked Al—the King did *too*.
Their wedding was a fabulous do!

One day a beggar knocked on *their* door.
"New lamps for old," he called with a roar.

"Aladdin's old lamp is a bit of a mess.
I'll swap it for a new one," said the princess.

It wasn't a beggar, but Wizard in disguise!
"The lamp is mine and much more besides!"

Wiz said, "Now genie, you must do what I say,
Take Al's wife and his palace far far away."

Aladdin soon followed on a fast horse.
He had *thought* up a clever plan, of course!

Al had a potion to make Wiz sleep for hours.
He took back the lamp and all of its powers.

On the way home, there was lots of laughter.
I believe they all lived happily ever after!

Can you find
11 pictures of
butterflies
in this story?

Puss in Boots

When *the* kindly miller grew old and died,
His *three* poor sons were sad and cried.

The mill soon belonged to the oldest son,
And the donkey was kept by the middle one.

That left the youngest with just the cat.
"What," he said, "is the good of that?"

But Puss said, "Just you buy for me,
Some boots and a bag and then you'll see."

Puss caught a hare. He went to the King,
Saying, "In this bag a present I bring."

Each day he took a fish or bird, and said,
"From the Duke of Carabas," bowing his head.

One day Puss saw the King approach,
With the Princess, in his grand coach.

"Jump in the lake," Puss said to the lad,
"Pretend to drown and shout like mad."

"Help my master," Puss cried to the King,
"Robbers took his clothes and stole everything."

The King's men took the boy from the water,
"You must introduce us," smiled his daughter.

The boy was soon dried and smartly dressed,
In the King's spare clothes, the very best.

On to a castle Puss swiftly ran,
In it lived an ogre. Puss had a plan!

Puss knocked on the door, scared by a shout,
He tried to look brave when the ogre came out.

"You're big," said Puss to the ogre of the house.
"Watch!" said Ogre and turned into a mouse.

With one blow, Puss killed the mouse dead. "This is our castle now, old ogre," he said.

The others arrived. Puss invited them in.
"Welcome home, Master," he said with a grin.

The boy understood. He smiled and bowed,
Looking most handsome, rich, and proud.

"The Duke of Carabas," Puss purred,
"And *this* is his castle, as you have heard."

The boy loved the Princess, she loved him too.
And so they got married without more ado.

They lived in the castle, so happy that
With them lived the boy's clever cat!